The Gingerbread Man

retold by VERA SOUTHGATE MA BCom

illustrated by PETER STEVENSON

Ladybird Books

Once upon a time, there was a little
old woman and a little old man.
They lived by themselves in a little
old house.

One day, the little old woman said
to the little old man, "I shall make
a gingerbread man.

"I shall make his eyes from two fat
currants, his nose and mouth from
bits of lemon peel and his coat
from sugar."

So the little old woman mixed the gingerbread.

She cut out the
little man's head,
his body, his arms
and his legs.

Then she patted them
out flat on a
baking tin.

Next she added two fat
currants for his eyes
and bits of lemon peel
for his nose and mouth.

And last of all,
she made his
coat from sugar.

9

The little old woman put the gingerbread man into the oven to bake. Then she went about her work.

Before long, it was time for the little gingerbread man to be cooked.

The little old woman went into the kitchen. But as she bent over the oven, she heard a tiny little voice.

"Let me out! Let me out!" it said.

The little old woman opened the oven door and as she did so, out popped the gingerbread man.

He hopped and skipped across the kitchen floor.

Then he ran right out of the kitchen door!

The little gingerbread man ran down the road and after him ran the little old woman and the little old man.

"Stop! Stop, little gingerbread man!" they cried.

But the little gingerbread man just looked back and cried,

"Run, run, as fast as you can,
You can't catch me,
I'm the gingerbread man!"

And they could not catch him.

The little gingerbread man ran on
and on. Soon he met a cow.

"Stop! Stop, little man!" said the
cow. "You look very good to eat."

But the little gingerbread man just
ran faster.

"I have run away from a little old woman and a little old man," cried the little gingerbread man. "I can run away from you, I can.

Run, run, as fast as you can,
You can't catch me,
I'm the gingerbread man!"

And the cow could not catch him.

The little gingerbread man ran on and on. Soon he met a horse.

"Stop! Stop, little man!" said the horse. "You look very good to eat."

But the little gingerbread man just
ran faster.

"I have run away from a little old woman, a little old man and a cow," cried the little gingerbread man. "I can run away from you, I can.

Run, run, as fast as you can,
You can't catch me,
I'm the gingerbread man!"

And the horse could not catch him.

The little gingerbread man ran on
and on. He began to feel very
proud of his running. "No one can
catch me," he cried.

Just then he met a sly old fox.

"Stop! Stop, little man!" said the
fox. "I want to talk to you."

"Oho! You can't catch me!" said the gingerbread man and he began to run faster.

The fox ran after the little gingerbread man. But the little gingerbread man ran faster still.

As he ran, the little gingerbread
man looked back and cried, "I
have run away from a little old
woman, a little old man, a cow and
a horse.

I can run away from you, I can.

Run, run, as fast as you can,

You can't catch me,

I'm the gingerbread man!"

"I don't want to catch you," said
the sly old fox. "I just want to talk
to you."

But the little gingerbread man kept on running. And the fox kept on running.

Soon the little gingerbread man came to a river. He stopped at the riverbank and the fox came running up.

"Oh! What shall I do?" cried the little gingerbread man. "I can't cross the river."

"Jump on my tail," said the sly old fox. "I will take you across the river."

So the little gingerbread man jumped onto the fox's tail. And the fox began to swim across the river.

Soon the fox turned his head and said, ''Little gingerbread man, you are too heavy for my tail. You will

get wet. Jump up onto my back.''

So the little gingerbread man

jumped onto the fox's back.

The sly old fox swam a little further
out into the river.

Then he turned his head again and
said, "Little gingerbread man, you
are too heavy for my back. You
will get wet. Jump onto my nose."

So the little gingerbread man
jumped onto the fox's nose.

Soon the fox reached the other side
of the river. The moment his feet
touched the
riverbank, he
tossed the
gingerbread man
into the air.

The fox opened
his mouth
and snap
went his
teeth.

"Oh dear!" said the little gingerbread man, "I am one quarter gone!"

Then he cried, "I am half gone!"

Then he cried, "I am three-quarters gone!"

And after that, the little gingerbread man said nothing more at all.